Chuck's Band

by Peggy Perry Anderson

Houghton Mifflin Company Boston 2008

Walter Lorraine Books

To Neice Janna
and Nephew Tyler

Walter Lorraine *wl* Books

www.houghtonmifflinbooks.com

Library of Congress Cataloging-in-Publication Data

Anderson, Peggy Perry.
  Chuck's band / by Peggy Perry Anderson.
      p. cm.
  "Walter Lorraine books."
  Summary: Chuck and his barnyard friends form a band, but they have trouble finding
an instrument for Fat Cat Pat to play, since all the cat wants to do is sleep all day.
  ISBN-13: 978-0-618-96506-9
  ISBN-10: 0-618-96506-8
  [1. Bands (Music)—Fiction. 2. Domestic animals—Fiction. 3. Stories in rhyme.] I. Title.
  PZ8.3.A5484Chp 2008
  [E]—dc22
                                                                    2007021728

Manufactured in Singapore
TWP 10 9 8 7 6 5 4 3 2 1

This is Chuck.

To town he went.

He bought a
musical instrument.

Here she
came, the
old goat Flo.
She heard
Chuck play his
new banjo.

Chuck bought her a mandolin.

Now Nip and Tuck
want to join in.

9

Tuck plays the guitar—
strum, strum,
strum! Nip plays harmonica—hum,
hum, hum!

The big cow Lou and the
little sow Sue wanted to
make some
music, too.

So Lou chose the washtub.
Thump, thump, thump!

Sue's little fiddle made her
dance and jump!

Huck the workhorse
heard the song.

With a bass violin

he could play along.

They played loudly, Sue and Lou,
Nip and Tuck, and Huck and Chuck.
"I heard your music!" quacked the
duck Luck.

The washboard
made a
rattling rap when
the duck Luck
pecked it.
Tap! Tap! Tap!

With a strum and a hum,
a peck and a pluck, they
all played a tune

while the chicken
went "cluck."

On the bucket
Buck could play.
Not only that, but
he could bray!

Fat Cat Pat came along with a pout.
Chuck didn't want her to feel left out.

Did she want this?
Did she want that?

Nothing seemed
right for Fat Cat Pat.

Meow! Meow!

What was that cat up to now?

Now Sue and
Lou and the goat
Flo too,

Nip and Tuck and the workhorse
Huck, the duck Luck, Chuck, and the
chicken that goes "cluck," along with
the braying burro Buck, can play!

And Fat Cat Pat
can sleep all day.